★ ENGELBERT ★
Joins the Circus

written by **TOM PAXTON**

illustrated by **ROBERTA WILSON**

Morrow Junior Books ★ NEW YORK

Egg tempera was used for the full-color illustrations.
The text type is 17-point Clearface.

Text copyright © 1997 by Tom Paxton
Illustrations copyright © 1997 by Roberta Wilson

Printed in Hong Kong by South China Printing Company (1988) Ltd.

1 2 3 4 5 6 7 8 9 10

Library of Congress Cataloging-in-Publication Data
Paxton, Tom.
Engelbert joins the circus/written by Tom Paxton; illustrated by Roberta Wilson.
p. cm.
Summary: After traveling from the jungle to America to visit his
cousin in the circus, Engelbert accidentally ends up in the spotlight and steals the show.
ISBN 0-688-09987-4 (trade)—ISBN 0-688-09988-2 (library)
[1. Elephants—Fiction.   2. Circus—Fiction.   3. Stories in rhyme.]
I. Wilson, Roberta, ill.   II. Title.   PZ8.3.P2738Em 1997   [E]—dc20   96-14835   CIP AC

To Mistofer Christopher
—T.P.

For my parents, Freda and Bill,
and to the memories of Sara and Barbara
—R.W.

A letter came for Engelbert
One steaming jungle day.
It reached him from America,
So very far away.
It came from Cousin Edgar,
Son of Hubert, brother of Nate.
He was working in the circus,
And his job was really great.

"Come join me in America!"
The letter rang with cheer.
"You'll love the circus life, I'm sure,
And you'll be welcome here."

So Engelbert set sail—
The vessel rocked from side to side.
Poor Engelbert! The ocean seemed
A million miles wide!

He landed just in time
To join the opening parade.
The band was playing marches—
What a stirring sight it made!
The clowns were all so funny there,
As through the town they went,
And everybody followed
To a quite enormous tent.

The circus folk were all around,
The noise was very loud,
While Engelbert was seeking
Cousin Edgar in the crowd.
Folks tried to squeeze around him—
Someone muttered, "Do you *mind*?"
Cousin Edgar, for an elephant,
Was very hard to find!

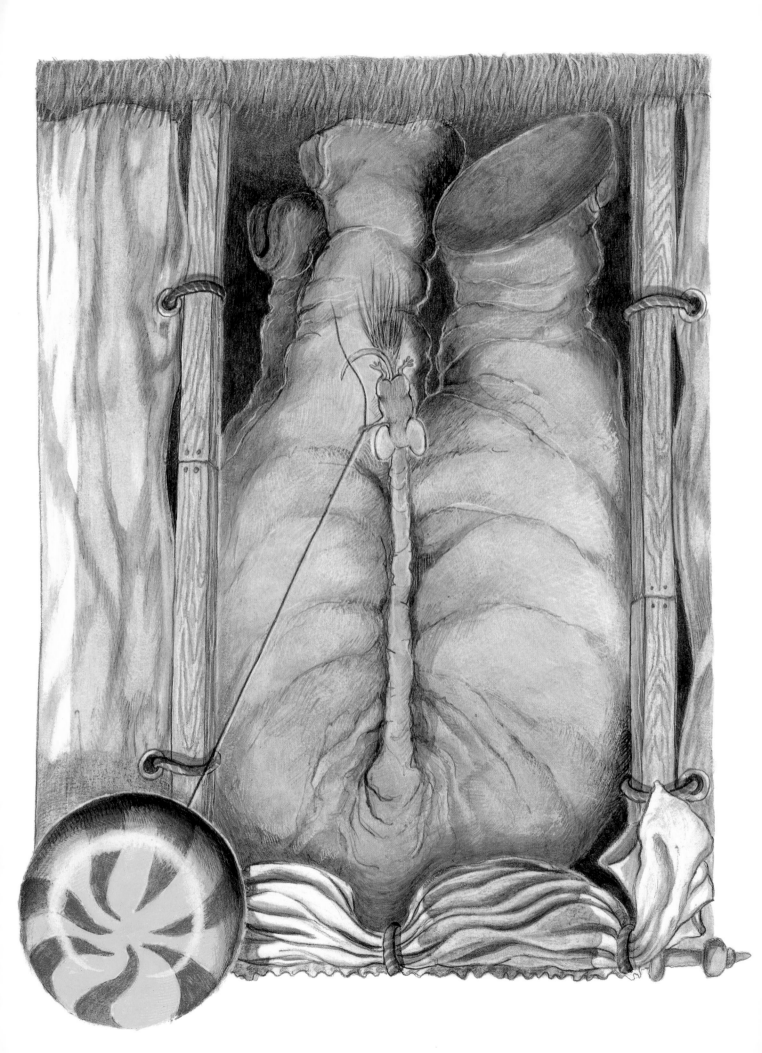

Then Engelbert saw Edgar
Disappearing through a door,
And as he tried to follow
He heard a sudden roar.

A spotlight shone down brightly
On the dusty circus floor.
But who stood in the spotlight?
It was Engelbert, for sure!

The performers were all horrified
To see him standing there.
"He'll ruin everything for us!"
Exclaimed the dancing bear.
The acrobats were furious,
The ringmaster was mad;
The strongman flexed his muscles,
And the smallest clown was sad.

But Engelbert was dazzled
By the music in the air,
And he started dancing slowly,
Moving gently here and there.
The crowd was so delighted
They craned their necks to peer.
For this dance came from far away,
And they'd *never* seen it here.

In front of Engelbert there stood
The lion tamer's chair.
He wrapped his trunk around it,
And he tossed it in the air.

Then, adding other pieces
To his juggling jamboree,
He flung them deftly skyward
For the startled crowd to see.

Then suddenly upon his back
There sprang the great Louise,
The queen of all the circus folk,
The star of the trapeze.
The band was playing beautifully
As round and round she spun,
With cheers and shouts of "Bravo!"
Ringing out from everyone.

Now the crowd was clapping
And the circus folk were glad.
This was the best performance
That the circus ever had.
And when the show was over,
The performers gathered near
And gave their thanks to Engelbert
With a rousing circus cheer.

So Engelbert agreed to stay
An extra week or so.
His special kind of juggling
Was the hit of every show.

BALLOONS
5¢

"I wish," said Cousin Edgar,
"You could stay with us for years.
Please promise you'll come back—
We never heard so many cheers."
Then Engelbert said, "Goodness,
What a splendid life you lead!
You bring such joy to people,
It's a ton of fun indeed.

"But I promised I'd go home,
And I'll be there awhile. Then,
Before you even miss me,
I'll come join you once again!"